D0042386
P7-ESD-987

TOP SHELF PRODUCTIONS
MARIETTA, GA

What is YOUR Secret Quest?

Published by Top Shelf Productions, PO Box 1282, Marietta, GA 30061-1282, USA. Top Shelf Productions is an imprint of IDW Publishing, a division of Idea and Design Works, LLC. Offices: 2765 Truxtun Road, San Diego, CA 92106. Top Shelf Productions®, the Top Shelf logo, Idea and Design Works®, and the IDW logo are registered trademarks of Idea and Design Works, LLC.

Editor-in-Chief: Chris Staros.

Edited by Leigh Walton.

Visit our online catalog at www.topshelfcomix.com.

Printed in Korea.

ISBN 978-1-60309-443-6

22 21 20 19 4 3 2 1

CHAPTER ONE

Boo!
Hello, Bushy!
I am Squiggle.

Silly Squiggle, my name is not Bushy.
It's not?

My name is Johnny Boo!
What?!

But... but... you look so different!
No, I don't.

But Johnny Boo has hair with a cool swoop-de-doo.
And yours is more like a big green FAWUZZLE.

Now you're just making stuff up to TEASE me.
No, I'm NOT.

So... FAWUZZLE is a Real word then?
I don't know, Johnny Boo. I can't even Read.
But it COULD be.

Well, I'm the KING and I say it's NOT a word.

King?!
flip!
I thought you said you were Johnny Boo!

I'm KING Johnny Boo!
poomf!
And this BUSH is my castle!

And as KING, I say-
FAWUZZLE is not a WORD.
No FAIR, Johnny Boo.

It's fair to ME!
Because I'm KING Johnny Boo!
HOORAY!

Oh, yeah?
Well, I'm KING SQUIGGLE!

And I say FAWUZZLE is a GREAT word!
Oh!

You can't be a king!
You don't have a CROWN.
Oh yeah?

Doomf!

TA-DA!

That's just a ROCK!
No, it isn't.
It's a CROWN.

Well, you still can't be King because you don't have a CASTLE.
But I do!

Mmm-hmm.
Where are you going?
ZIP

I've got a big FAWUZZLE castle!
Hey, NO FAIR!

CHAPTER TWO

I WIN, JOHNNY Boo. Fawuzzle fawuzzle!
But you cheated, Squiggle!
No faiR.

I was KiNg fiRST!
AND I alReady said FAWUZZLE is NOT a WORD.

But I'm KiNg Squiggle, and I have the BIGGEST castle.

So, King Squiggle says-
FAWUZZLE is the ONLY word!
What?!! NO!!

Fawuzzle fawuzzle FAWUZZLE.

It can't be the ONLY word.
That's silly.

How would you say "hello"?
Fawuzzle.

Then how about "goodbye"?
Fawuzzle!

Okay, that kinda makes sense.
Like "aloha."

But what if you wanted to say "I'm going to ride my bicycle to the sun and boil a million hot dogs in melted ice cream"?
What then?

I'd say-
Fawuzzle fawuzzle fawuzzle fawuzzle fawuzzle fawuzzle fawuzzle fawuzzle fawuzzle fawuzzle fawuzzle fawuzzle fawuzzle fawuzzle fawuzzle fawuzzle fawuzzle fawuzzle FAWUZZLE!!
See?
Squiggle! That's TOO MANY FAWUZZLES!

No more fawuzzles! The end.

Fawuzzle?
No!

Snif

WAAAA!
flip

WAAAAA!
Oops.
DOOMP

WAAAA!

WAAAAA!
Gosh.

King Johnny Boo doesn't LIKE crying!!
Noooo.

WAAAAAA!

WAAAA!

Excuse me, King Squiggle.
You dropped Rocky the Rock.
POOMF
Waa- huh?
Rocky says he wants to be your crown.
So... Ta-da!
I'm sorry I cried, Johnny Boo.

Don't worry, Squiggle.
You know what they say...
No, Johnny Boo. What do they say?

Fawuzzle!
Ha ha!
So true.

CHAPTER THREE

And now we're sharing!
SHARE SHARE SHARE!
Sharing is cool!
Share Share SHARE!

Waaa! That's not FAIR!
Huh?
It's the ICE CREAM MONSTER!
flap flap flap
flap flap

WAAAA!
You guys!
You're being MEAN to me!

No, we're not.
We're just sitting here, sharing-

Sharing is NOT FAIR!
WAAAA!

It's not?
Oh no!

You guys are having a BIG ice cream party in the SKY!
And you're WASTING the ice cream by SHARING it instead of giving all the ice cream to ME!
WAAA! No FAIR!!

CHAPTER FOUR

These are our CROWNS!
Mine is also a ROCK. Ta-da!

TRICKS! Also, I can see you sitting in a big blob of green ice cream!
I SEE it!

Silly Ice Cream Monster. This is just our castle!
It is also a tree.
TRICKY TRICKS!
You're tricky-tricking me!

I want ice cream on my head too!
I want to SIT in an ICE CREAM CASTLE!

That's good, Ice Cream Monster. Just use your imagination.
Like we do!

Oh my!
No! I want it to be REAL!
RAR!
CRACK

ICE CREAM ON my HEAD!!
DOOMF

Here we go, I guess!
Me too!
Now I'll go find a REAL ice cream castle to SIT IN.
Stomp stomp
Stomp!

CHAPTER FIVE

Where should we fly to, King Johnny Boo?

Anywhere we want! Hooray!
Wow!

Anywhere in the WHOLE WORLD?
Sure.

Even the MOON?!

ESPECIALLY the MOON!
Wow, oh wow!

Then what are we waiting for, Johnny Boo?
Let's hurry up and go!

Let's zoom zoom ZOOM!
To the MOON!

Tee hee. This reminds me of my famous adventure "Johnny Boo Zooms to the Moon."
But this time, I am awake.
Also, we are kings!

Wait a minute... why did we stop?
Did we Reach the moon already?

That's not the moon, King Squiggle, that's-
Ice cream!

FINALLY! I found my ice CREAM castle...

...to Sit iN...
Nooooo!
With my BUTT!

I am SO HAPPY!
I'm sitting in a REAL castle made of ICE CREAM and not using my IMAGINATION!
SQUISH
My big BOTTOM is the KING of the ICE CREAM!

Happy happy happy!
Still?
We've been sitting here for HOURS.

Also, BORED.
Yawn!

So happy sleepy bored.
DROOP

Our flying castle fell asleep.
Oops.
ZZZZ...

Come on.
JUMP

Should we wake him up?
ZZZ

No...
ZZZZ
He looks so peaceful.

Right?
Heh heh. Yeah! He is kind of cute and stuff when he isn't yelling "RAR!"
ZZZ.

Silly sleepy flying castle.
Good Night.
PAT PAT
Z

Now, shhhh...
Shhh...
Shhh.

I kind of want to yell BOO really loud.
Don't do it, Johnny Boo. You'll wake him up.

Just tip-toe away.
No yelling BOO.

Tip toe tip toe tip toe...
Tip too top tea toe tup-

ZZZ.
Tippy tap tay -wait a minute!!

My secret quest is COMPLETE!

What is it, King Johnny Boo?
It is this!

The mighty sword of King Johnny Boo...
The sword named... Excaliboo!
Wow!

CHAPTER SEVEN

That's okay!
He likes it.
His whole body is like a helmet.

Now... en garde! Sword fight!
CLANG

Take that!
And that!
CLANG CLANG
Take this!
And this!
CLANG
CLAN

CLANG
I wonder why the Ice Cream Monster got so sleepy?
King Squiggle is WIDE AWAKE!

He probably got tired out on his long journey to the moon.
CLANG
Oh yeah.

Wait. We went all the way to the moon?
I didn't notice.

Just look up in the sky, Squiggle!
See?
Planet Earth is far away.
Wow!

Actually, wow isn't the right word.
Then what's the right word?

Amazing? Wonderful? Cute? Roundy? Silly? Pumpkin-pie? Ostrich-britches? George?
No, Johnny Boo-

Fawuzzle!
Ha ha! Good word!
THE END

ZzZ...
Z.